E
De   Decker, Dorothy W
      Stripe presents the ABC's.

DATE DUE

SE 18 '85	MY 15 '89	MY 26 '93
OC 2 '85	SE 16 '89	SEP 22 '95
OC 23 '85	OC 2 '89	JAN 21 '97
FE 7 '86	NO 8 '89	FEB 20 '97
SE 14 '88	AP 26 '90	AG 21 '02
MY 7 '88	JE 28 '90	JA 28 '06
JY 1 '86	AG 15 '90	FE 09 '06
SE 13 '86	AG 21 '90	MR 20 '06
JY 28 '88	OC 23 '90	JY 1 6 '10
AG 16 '88	JY 20 '92	
SE 9 '88	JY 30 '92	
MR 10 '89	DE 1 7 '92	

DEMCO

the
ABC's

STRIPE
presents the
ABC's

Written and Illustrated by Dorothy W. Decker

Gemstone Books

DILLON PRESS, INC. MINNEAPOLIS, MN 55415

Library of Congress Cataloging in Publication Data

Decker, Dorothy.
  Stripe presents the ABC's.

  Summary: Stripe the Bear romps through the alphabet presenting
the letters in upper and lower case and sign language, and disclos-
ing some facts about animals.
  1. English language—Alphabet—Juvenile literature. 2. Sign language—Juvenile literature. [1. Alphabet. 2. Animals—Miscel-
lanea. 3. Sign language] I. Title. II. Title: Stripe presents the
ABC's.
PE1155.D42   1984   [E]   84-12180
ISBN 0-87518-266-6

Dillon Press, Inc.   242 Portland Avenue South
Minneapolis, Minnesota 55415

Printed in the United States of America
1 2 3 4 5 6 7 8 9 10 92 91 90 89 88 87 86 85 84

This book is about the twenty-six letters of the Roman alphabet. It will help you learn the capital and small forms of each letter. It will also show you how to make these letters in the manual alphabet by using your hand and fingers.

Hello! My name is Stripe, and I have some pictures I'd like to show you. They're from a trip I took a short while ago. Please turn the page if you'd like to see them.

Aa

Here I am with an **ape**. I met him while I was on safari in the jungle. He can walk around on two feet or on all fours. He likes to eat leaves and fruit, especially bananas.

 # Bb

One night I was awakened by a noise. When I went outside, I looked up and saw a **bat** flying overhead. Did you know that bats sleep during the day, hanging upside down? At night, when you're sleeping, they play flying games and hunt for food.

13

This picture shows me sitting on a **camel** in the Egyptian desert. Camels have long eyelashes to protect their eyes from the blowing sand. I had to wear sunglasses to keep the sand out of mine.

Dd

My **dog** Steve likes to go for walks in the park. Sometimes he pulls on his leash because he wants to run. I use the leash so that he won't run off and get lost.

When I was in Washington, D.C., where the president lives, I visited a big museum. In this picture I'm looking at a painting of the American **eagle**. This great bird is a symbol, or sign, of the United States of America.

One day, when I was going for a walk, I saw a **frog** resting on a lily pad in a pond. I think he was waiting for a snack to fly by. His long hind legs enable him to jump great distances.

Gg

When I went to the Animal Park, I gave this **giraffe** a big leaf to eat. Her neck is so long that she can feed on the leaves that grow at the tops of trees. She can also go without a drink of water for a long time.

This **horse**, named Lobo, took me for a long ride. When we got back, I put him in his stall. Horses eat hay and oats and treats such as apples and carrots.

Down in Mexico, I met an **iguana**. He told me that he can grow to be six feet long. I also learned that if he gets angry or excited, he changes color from yellow to red-orange.

J j

I managed to get a good picture of this **jaguar** in South America. I didn't want him to see me because jaguars can be very dangerous. They are not afraid of anything. Sometimes they even jump into the water to catch crocodiles!

K k

In Australia I went for a ride with a **kangaroo**. I sat in the pouch where she usually carries her babies. Traveling this way was quite comfortable.

While staying in a city, I saw a
statue of a **lion** at the main library.
Real lions live in groups called
prides. They do little more than
sleep, hunt, and eat.

This little **mouse** lives in a cottage in Ireland. I peeked through his door to see him sitting down to dinner. He was having cheese and cracker bits.

Nn

Here I am in *Lilbo*, my boat, watching a **narwhal** *(NAHR hwuhl)* splash about in the Arctic Ocean. These whales aren't seen very often. They have dark-gray or black spots and grow a long ivory tusk.

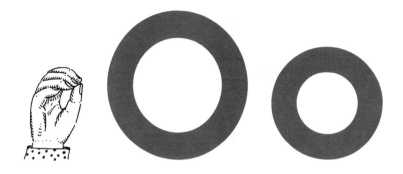

I climbed a tree to visit this **owl**. He told me that he flies at night and sleeps during the day. I said I was sorry for waking him and promised to come back later.

On my way to a party, I met an emperor **penguin** named Bruce. He told me that he was on his way to help care for some newborn chicks. Grown-up emperor penguins spend lots of time with their young. They are also good swimmers, although we usually see pictures of them standing on land.

41

One day I saw a **quail** family taking
a stroll. They were led by their father,
who has pretty, colorful feathers.

R r

Near the North Pole, I asked directions from one of Santa Claus's **reindeer**. He likes working for Santa and looks forward to December 25. Reindeer don't mind cold weather, and they are very good at pulling heavy loads.

S s

I was enjoying a picnic in the English countryside when this **squirrel** stopped to chat. While I ate my sandwich and cookies, she nibbled on a walnut.

This **tortoise** and I met in the Arizona desert. He had just gotten up from his nap. When the sun is very hot, tortoises stay in their cool holes and sleep. Their favorite food is a cactus plant—without the needles.

U u

In a magical forest, I found a very beautiful **unicorn**. She told me that there are those who don't believe in unicorns. I told her I did.

V v

I was snug and warm in my sleeping bag when I spotted this **vulture** perched in an old dead tree. He never spoke a word. He just looked down hungrily at me.

On an expedition in the Arctic, I met a big old **walrus**. He told me that he liked taking sunbaths. As you can see, walrus have long tusks. They use them to break the ice and to protect their families.

X x

I was exploring the underwater world when I swam right into a member of the **xiphias** *(ZIF y ahs)*, or swordfish, family. He had a long bill, or jaw, which I was careful to avoid. He told me that he had just eaten a meal of fish and squid. He also said that he likes to swim where the water is warm.

Yy

High in the mountains of Asia, I talked with this **yak**. I told her I thought her long, thick hair was very pretty. She thanked me and said that it kept her nice and warm in the freezing cold weather.

On my last stop I visited the plains of Africa. Here I met a friendly **zebra**. When I told her my name, she started to giggle. "You are Stripe, and I am striped," she said. Then we both started to laugh. What a nice way to end my trip!

Stripe Presents the ABC's is Dorothy Decker's first book. Yet Stripe himself has lived in her imagination for several years. In fact, he was born "on an evening in November of 1981." "[While] sitting at my drawing table," she writes, "I noticed that one of our [toy] bears was standing on the edge of the sofa. He actually looked as if he were about to jump off. I interrupted my work to make several sketches. From these, his first portrait was painted."

When she is not busy creating more adventures for Stripe, Ms. Decker works as a free-lance artist in New York City. A painter by training, she is a graduate of the Otis-Parsons Art Institute, which granted her a Bachelor of Fine Arts degree.